Davey McGravy

Davey McGravy

*Tales to Be Read Aloud
to Children and Adult Children*

David Mason

Illustrations by Grant Silverstein

PAUL DRY BOOKS
Philadelphia 2015

First Paul Dry Books Edition, 2015

Paul Dry Books, Inc.
Philadelphia, Pennsylvania
www.pauldrybooks.com

Library of Congress Cataloging-in-Publication Data
Mason, David, 1954–
   Davey McGravy / David Mason ; illustrations by Grant Silverstein.
      pages cm
   Summary: Davey McGravy, who mourns his missing mother every day,
finds solace in nature, his imagination, and the love of his father and
brothers.
   ISBN 978-1-58988-099-3 (paperback)
   [1. Novels in verse. 2. Single-parent families—Fiction. 3. Nature—Fiction.
4. Flight—Fiction.] I. Silverstein, Grant, illustrator. II. Title.
   PZ7.5.M38Dav 2015
   [Fic]—dc23
                                                    2014025300

For Cally (Chrissy)
the Namer . . .

Contents

McG

....

To Love

May I call you Love?

Very well, then, you are Love,
and this is a tale about a boy
named Davey.

Never mind the rest of his name.
You need only know he was born
in the land of rain
and the tallest of tall trees—

great shaggy cedars like the boots
of giants covered in green,
and where the giants had gone
no one could ever tell.

Only their boots remained
on the wet green grass,
surrounded by ferns on the shore
of a long, cold, windy lake.

That's where Davey was born, Love.
That's where you must imagine him,
a wee squall of tears and swaddling,
a babe, as you too were a babe,

with parents and the whole canoe,
the whole catastrophe
we call a family—
the human zoo.

~ Sometimes wind was a stream ~

The Whole Catastrophe

First there was Big Brother
who hated the day Davey was born.
Then there was Little Brother,
not happy Davey got there before.

Ah well, our Davey was a plucky lad—
lad was a word they used in the faraway
of Davey's dreams, the place
of giant trees and rainy mountains.

Some days when he was little
he thought he saw the giants
outside in the woods, looking,
looking for their lost boots.

Big Brother said, "That's stupid."
Little Brother said, "What's a giant?"
So Davey looked and kept to himself
the secret of what he saw.

Sometimes in the woods
he heard the trees complain
(the way wind made them creak)
of all their aches and pains.

Sometimes wind was a stream
far, far up in the trees
and birds went swimming through the air
wherever they pleased.

Big Brother said, "Don't say that."
Little Brother sucked his thumb.
"You can't say crazy things like that,"
Big Brother said, "it's dumb."

Sometimes Davey saw faces
looking in the windows at him.
His brothers looked at Davey
as if he was so dim,

or maybe a little bit crazy
and certainly kinda dumb.
Big Brother said, "Don't say that."
Little Brother sucked his thumb.

Sometimes being the middle child
is saddening!
Always second fiddle!
Maddening!

More of the Catastrophe

And must I tell you, Love,
There was a mother too?
Oh, there was.
Indeed there was.

And she was beautiful.
She came to the Land of Rain
from a faraway place of rock
beside a great brown river.

When Davey came to her alone
she reached to touch his hair
and smiled at him, then looked away
with a far-off stare.

Oh, do I need to tell you, Love
that mother was not long for this world?
Do I need to tell you how
she fell into a fog and left?

"What's a fog?" Little Brother asked.
"Don't ask," Big Brother said.
But Davey saw his mother go away
and heard what doctors had to say.

And when he went outside
he tried to play beside
the giant boots on the grass,
and tried to listen to the lake,

to hear waves laughing
as they passed.
But that day even water was sad.
That day everyone felt very bad.

~ *We cannot always know where our mothers go.* ~

Ah well, these things come to pass.
We cannot always know
where our mothers go.
And Davey lived, and Davey grew.

Still More Catastrophe!

The trees cast long shadows
on the lawn beside the lake,
and the dew-cold grass was like a bed
of tears where Davey walked

barefoot at morning.
Davey was mourning
and his brothers mourned
but they could not mourn forever . . .

So they ran beside the lake
on the dew-cold grass,
and left the shadows of the trees
for the warmth of the morning sun,

boys on the run,
boys in the day,
ready to swim
and ready to play.

Oh, yes—

Still More

—there was still more.

"Where's Mom?" Little Brother asked.
"Shut up," Big Brother said.
The giants will find her, thought Davey.

He looked into a bramble
where berries hung like night,
and wondered where the stars went
in the broad daylight.

He raised his eyes and stared
across the lake to hills
where mist was rising like wet smoke
among the glistening firs.

"Look, there's an otter in the lake!"
He pointed, but his brothers didn't see
the long slippery body
slide away under a wave.

"I saw it. I saw!" Davey shouted.
"You didn't see anything," Big Brother said,
and he punched Davey's arm.
"What's an otter?" Little Brother asked.

Our father is an otter,
Davey thought, *and swims
in waves, worrying,
and dives under for hours.*

What's wrong with me? he wondered.
*I see things nobody sees.
So many things are waving
like tall ferns in a breeze.*

~ *"Look, there's an otter in the lake!"* ~

While his brothers ran
by the shore, Davey looked
back to the giant boots and the house,
the green walls of the house,

and the windows, dark,
and he knew
his father was home from work,
and he knew what he had to do.

Father Was Home from Work

Yes, Love, there was a father.
Sad father with his freckles
and whiskers. Oh yes.
And you must remember this:

The father loved his boys,
and though his wife had gone away
in a fog with talking doctors,
he thought of them, his boys.

He thought of them when he was at work
in the woods with his big axe.
He thought of them when he fished
and brought home the catch.

He thought of them when he fried
the caught trout in a pan
and looked out the darkened windows
at the lake beside the land.

The Screen Door

Davey went up the steps
and opened the screen door wide
and heard the hinges creak
when he went inside.

He smelled the cooking smell
of trout in the frying pan
and knew his otter father
was home. And sad.

He saw his boots beside the door,
his jacket hung on the hook
and went inside the kitchen
to watch his father cook.

His father was a giant
with whiskers and freckled arms
who stood in the kitchen in stocking feet,
humming an old hymn

or a chantey learned in the Navy,
or a song from the radio.
And Davey looked at his father
and knew what he had to do.

The Kitchen

He walked to where his father stood
and hugged him by a leg
and wept like the babe he used to be
in the green house by the lake.

He wept for the giants in the woods,
for the otter that swam in the waves.
He wept for his mother in the fog
so far away.

And then he felt a hand,
a big hand on his hair.
"It's Davey McGravy," his father said.
"I'm glad you're here."

"Davey McGravy," he said again,
"How's that for a brand new name?
Davey McGravy. Not so bad.
I like a name that rhymes."

And there was his father on his knees
holding our boy in his arms.
And Davey McGravy felt the scratch
of whiskers and felt warm.

"Nobody else has a name like that.
It's all your own.
Davey McGravy. Davey McGravy.
You could sing it in a song."

And then his father kissed him,
ruffled his hair and said,
"Supper time, Davey McGravy.
Then it's time for bed."

~ He walked to where his father stood and hugged him by a leg ~

A Brand-New Name

Love—
I'm so glad I can call you Love—
do you know what Davey felt?
He felt his sadness like a friend.

Davey McGravy, Davey McGravy,
a name to conjure with,
to dream with by the cedar trees
out in the rainy woods.

A name his father gave him
just like that, on a day
when no one else saw the otter
dive in the waves at play.

When no one else believed him,
or even liked him much,
his father gave him a brand new name
and a loving touch.

Supper!

The trout looked pretty unhappy
fried in the frying pan,
but three boys and their father
ate it right down.

They ate it with potatoes
and two or three green beans.
Little Brother pushed his beans about.
Big Brother complained.

But Davey couldn't remember
what he ate that night.
He was singing his name in a secret song
when his father turned out the light.

Father kissed each of his boys
and tucked them in for sleep,
but said no word of their mother
for fear he would weep.

The Moon on the Lake

Love, do you ever pretend
you have gone asleep?
Davey was singing his secret song,
and that kept him up.

Davey McGravy, Davey McGravy,
a name to conjure with.
I like a name that rhymes,
and waves like waves on the lake.

It sounds like rain on a window.
It sounds like wind in the trees.
It sounds like a fern in the forest
waving in the breeze.

Outside his window the moon
hung over the giant boots
and painted the waves with a path of light
far out beyond the boats.

And maybe out there somewhere
his mother would learn his name

and smile because she knew him
just the same.

For now it was his secret,
his own name, and it rhymed,
and his father had given it to him
for all of time.

As he fell to sleep the water
and moon were whispering
over the giant boots
and Davey was singing:

It sounds like rain on a window.
It sounds like wind in the trees.
It sounds like a fern in the forest
waving in the breeze.

Davey's
Blue Monday

Do You Remember?

Love, do you remember
the green-walled house by the lake
in the land of rain
and the tallest of tall trees?

Remember the three boys
whose mother went away,
how their father came home and sang
Davey McGravy's name?

Davey McGravy, Davey McGravy,
a name to conjure with,
to dream with by the cedar trees
out in the rainy woods.

Remember it made him happy
to have his brand-new name
sung to him by his father
and shimmered by the moon?

Love—I'm so glad I can call you Love!
Isn't it good to be here like this,
telling another story
about our boy by the lake?

Nothing to Do

It was a blue Monday
and Davey had nothing to do,
and his brothers, too,
had nothing to do.

It was summer—no school!—
but the sky was heavy,
a gray-blue day,
and Davey felt it in his bones.

Big Brother glued a model ship.
Little Brother sat on the floor.
"Stay away from my ship," Big Brother said.
Davey walked out the door.

The screen door clattered behind his back,
but in front lay all the world,
the cedar trees, the ferns, the lake
lovely and wild.

Beyond the silver waves the hills
were dark, dark green, and the mist
rose up like smoke from the trees,
and the air was damp with the lightest breeze.

The sun was hiding or asleep,
and blue-gray Monday waited there
for someone like Davey to notice it.
He stood on the grass and stared.

And then—

The Woods

—he took a step, and another step,
and the air came and wrapped around him,
and his skin felt alive and somewhat cold
in all the world abounding.

Everything was moving now.
The trees waved. On the lake
waves rose and fell
but the blue-gray sky was still.

And the world said, "Now."
And Davey McGravy knew
that everything was now,
now in the damp, now in the blue,

now in the green and the darker green,
the leaves and stems and sticks,
now in the house where his brothers sat,
now in the woods where his father worked,

now in the mist where his mother had gone,
where giants lost their boots,
now in the ducks on the tossing waves,
now in the nodding boats.

Now, now, all is now.
He was walking into the woods
where the ferns were now and the green salal
rose up in its shiny bush.

How could it be
the day was quiet?
Nobody talked, and yet a riot
of beings were moving and alive.

He tried to walk with silent steps,
but the twigs snapped "Ouch!" and the nettles sighed,
and the tall trees rose
on every side

until the woods were darker than dark
and something touched his face—

a spider web that crossed the path!
He'd made a tattered space

and the spider ran down the sticky thread
to build her web again.
Davey ducked under the web and walked
so as not to disturb his friend.

The touch of the web stayed with him, though,
light as a breath,
and the dew on the leaves ran off on his jeans,
and his shoes were soaking wet.

He followed the narrow trail where it led.
The leaves and trees grew dense,
and far above the highest boughs
waved in their gentle dance.

Now, now, all is now.
Was it Davey who thought the words
or was it the air, the dew, the highest boughs
up with the swimming birds?

He looked ahead at the turning path.
*Just one more turn, and I'll see
what's around the bend*, he thought,
after that next tall tree.

Around the Bend

He stepped over a root at the foot of a yew,
and the trail went on beyond,
and Davey stood on the dark, wet path,
and thought about what he'd seen.

His breath went into the day like mist.
The woods were breathing too.
An owl was talking somewhere ahead:
"Who? To-who? To-who?"

And a raven answered,
"Now, now, now."
And Davey looked ahead,
wondering if he should go.

And that was when he saw them—red
or orangey-red in their dozens,
the most delicate shrub he'd ever seen,
loaded with huckleberries!

His father had shown him what to eat
in the woods, what he should avoid.
Thimbleberries were good, of course,
blackberries with their thorns,

and salmonberries—yum-yum-yum—
but the rarest berries of all
were the tiny, tiny huckleberries.
they looked like salmon roe,

but they tasted tart,
tart and sweet, sweet and tart.
He ran to the shrub with its delicate leaves
and the berries at its heart.

He filled his fists with the little fruits,
and then he filled his mouth,
and squished them and enjoyed the juice
and swallowed the berries down.

He hadn't known he was hungry that day.
Big Brother had made toast.

~ He filled his stomach with tart and sweet ~

Little Brother ate a banana.
But Davey just got lost.

Lost in the woods with the now and the owl
and the huckleberry bush.
He filled his stomach with tart and sweet,
and felt blue Monday was complete,
nowhere to go, no one to meet,
and there was no rush.

But after a while . . .

And Another Bend

. . . he wanted to see around the bend,
and another bend after that,
and the winding trail went on through the woods,
and walking lightened his heart.

It was good to be alone.
No brothers to tell him he was dumb
for saying what he saw,
alone with his rhyming name.

He could stay in the woods all day if he wished
and when his father came home
at the end of day with another fish
Davey would be home too.

And he wasn't really lost in the woods.
He heard the lake behind him
and saw the trail ahead,
winding and winding.

He stepped on a giant cedar log,
wet and rotting on the ground.
The wood was soft beneath his shoes
and made a squishy sound,

so he stopped and touched it with his hand,
and saw his skin dyed red.
This is what happens to trees, he thought,
when they are dead.

They fall apart in the forest
until they become like dirt,
a wet hotel for beetles,
and it doesn't really hurt.

The lake at his back was quiet now.
The mist high up in the trees
was like wet smoke from an ancient fire
back in the giants' days.

Somewhere ahead was another sound
of water in the woods,
and beyond that sound was the strangest call
Davey had ever heard.

The Waterfall

He followed the water sound—
that's often a good idea—
and the trail turned up a hill
and the dark woods suddenly cleared,

and there was a cliff of smooth wet rock,
and a splashing pool, and above the pool

a glimmering waterfall
so clear and cool,

like quiet laughter in the day
falling from above.
The water fell and mosses clung
to the rocks like love.

Old logs lay across the stream.
Mosses loved them too.
Davey McGravy laughed at the sight,
and knew what he had to do.

He climbed on a wet log over the pool
and hugged the trunk like his father's leg
and lay with his cheek on a pillow of moss
to watch the water bugs.

He watched them move on the surface
and then saw deeper in
where minnows darted among the rocks,
so pale and thin.

Now, now, all is now,
said the quiet voice within.
And then the strangest thing he'd ever heard—
that call again.

Beyond the laughing waterfall,
beyond the waving trees,
beyond the shifting of the rocks,
a high-pitched, plaintive "Please!"

And "Hear, hear, hear,"
and "Please!"
The strangest call he'd ever heard
was carried on the breeze.

The King of the Fir Trees

It wasn't quite a whistle.
Nor was it really a squawk.
The last thing Davey expected to see
in the woods was a peacock!

But there it sat in a fir tree
not twenty feet away!
This blue Monday was proving to be
an extraordinary day.

The peacock perched on a fir bough,
lording it over the woods,
its blue head calling, "Please!" and "Hear!"
perfectly understood.

And rising behind the peacock
from a most magnificent tail,
a fan of eyes were watching
the boy by the waterfall.

Davey sat up with a start.
He straddled the log and looked
at the feathered king of the fir trees.
For a moment his body shook.

"What do you want me to hear?" he asked.
"Did you run off from a farm,
or how did you ever get here?"
The bird said, "Don't be alarmed."

Or maybe it said nothing.
Maybe it was the breeze.
Maybe the bird was calling,
"Please, oh please, oh please!"

But the way it puffed out its breast
and the way its eyes looked on
at the boy on the log by the waterfall
was something to think upon.

Why shouldn't a peacock talk
if there's somebody present to listen?
Maybe the whole world is talking
and people just miss it.

"Oh please," the bird said again.
And "Don't be alarmed, my boy.
Finding a peacock in the firs
should fill you with joy."

Davey stood up on the log
and crossed to the bank of the stream
and sat on a mossy stone.
Was this a dream?

Was he napping beside the water?
Was he walking in his sleep?
Had the whole of this blue Monday
never been his to keep?

"Don't fret over that," said the bird,
who must have read his thought.
"Everything always happens
as if it had not.

"Am I real or aren't I?
Don't you believe my eyes?
I'm the king of the fir trees
and these are my spies!"

With that the bird fanned out his tail
in a shimmering feather-rainbow

and stared with all of his eyes
at little Davey below.

The Peacock Talks

"I know who you are," said the bird.
"You're the boy with a rhyming name.
I think I've been dreaming of you
in your house by the lake.

"My eyes are a kind of rhyme—can you see?
Side by side and nearly the same.
I have rainbow eyes.
Do you think it will rain?

"And rain is a kind of rhyme,
and so are two halves of a leaf.
And maybe you walked out in the woods
to rhyme away your grief."

"Where is my mother?" Davey asked,
as rain began to fall
from the blue-gray clouds above the woods.
The drops were cold and small.

"Lost in a fog," the peacock said.
"But nothing is really lost.
Look at the trees in the forest
beloved by the moss.

"Davey McGravy—quite a name,
and I see it fits you well.
You're a boy who rhymes and a boy who sees things
clear as a bell."

~ *The peacock talks* ~

The rain fell heavier from the cloud
and danced on the minnow pool,
and water on the mossy rocks
fell and fell and fell.

"It's late," said the bird. "You should go home.
Your father will soon be back,
and day will end and night will come,
moonless and black.

"Remember your name, my boy.
Remember who you are.
Remember the forest sees you.
And when there are no stars

"remember the web that touched you
light as a mother's touch,
your meal of huckleberries,
the moss like a couch.

"And when your brothers are grumpy,
constantly calling you dumb,
when Big Brother says 'Don't say that,'
and Little Brother sucks his thumb,

"there's somewhere you won't be lonely,
the waterfall out in the woods.
And maybe you'll talk to a peacock
and find yourself understood!

"Most likely you won't," said the bird.
"I'm old, and I realize
it isn't every day you meet
a bird with two hundred eyes."

At that the bird unfanned its tail
and closed both eyes in its head.

"Time for us both to go back to our homes,"
the nodding peacock said.

The Green House

Wherever the sun was hiding,
Davey could tell it was late.
It was almost dark on the path
when he made his way back to the lake,

away from the falling water,
soaked to his skin by the rain,
over the rotting cedar tree
and under the web again

with another handful of berries
sweet and tart in his mouth,
and his eyes were getting heavy
as he walked vaguely south.

And then a clearing opened
where rain fell onto the house,
on all the nodding fishing boats
and the lake at peace.

And there was his father unloading the truck,
turning to see his son.
"Hey there, Davey McGravy,
where have you been?

"You can tell me over supper,
but first let's get you dry.
You must be growing tougher
if the wet doesn't make you cry.

"Davey McGravy," his father said.
"I like a name that rhymes."
And Love, that was the way our Davey
knew he was at home.

Davey
Learns to Fly

There Were Neighbors

Love, does it seem the green house
was far from any town?
Well, it was not so far as that,
but it seemed far in Davey's mind.

Sometimes things feel distant
when they're not—isn't that true?
But Davey knew the world was large
and Monday was always blue.

And sometimes things that are truly far
seem near at hand. When Davey thought
of his mother lost in a fog
he could see her out on a boat

and see her in the house and see her
in the garden bending to plant.
He could see the way she looked at him.
He could see her beautiful hands.

It was like a dream, as real as a dream,
the way the peacock talked to him,
the way one Saturday he woke up
but stayed in bed on a whim.

And through his open window
he heard the lapping lake,
and out in the yard his father
and Mr. Larsen talked.

Mr. Larsen was a neighbor
from over the woods toward town.
The two men were cutting lumber
below on the lawn.

Davey got dressed and went downstairs,
the dark stairs leading down
from the dim-lit hall,
feeling the dark on his skin.

In the kitchen Big Brother sat,
gluing his model ship,
while Little Brother played,
making motor sounds with his lips.

Outside Davey felt the sun
warming the dark from his bones,
while his father and Mr. Larsen
sawed the two-by-fours.

He smelled the fresh-cut lumber
and Mr. Larsen's pipe
and the warming grass below his feet.
And all of last night's sleep

went out in the summer day to live
wherever sleeping goes,
where shadows gather under leaves
and the lightest breezes blow.

"*Ja*, Davey," Mr. Larsen said.
"Your dad is building a fence
around the vegetable patch.
It makes good sense

to keep the deer from feeding
on everything you grow."
So Davey watched them cutting wood
as the sawdust fell like snow,

and he thought of his mother's garden
where she used to kneel and plant

and pull up weeds from the dark, rich soil
with her beautiful hands.

Sometimes things that are truly far
seem close—you can almost see
whatever you miss as real
as a peacock in a tree.

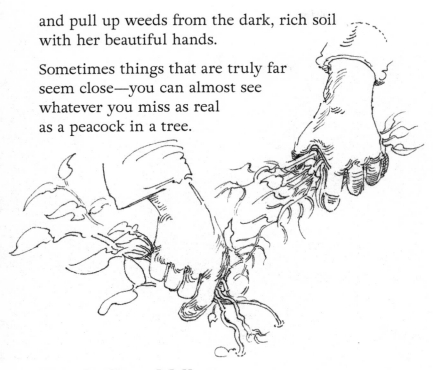

The Rolling Hill

Behind the vegetable patch was a hill
where the grass was left unmowed.
Its tall stems leaned with the weight of seeds
and the sunstruck dew was gold.

The perfect hill for rolling
on days when the wind blew warm.
Davey rolled down it many times
and never came to harm

because the grass embraced him
and the dew was soft and damp
and the sun climbed over the rolling hill
like a giant lamp

and the nearby trees were sighing
and brambles hummed with bees
and Davey was free to roll down the hill
as many times as he pleased.

He rolled on his side like a log
and saw the world spin around.
The wind went whoosh in his ears
with a flying sound.

The grass bent down beneath him,
smelling so damp and sweet.
Davey lay and felt the day
was utterly complete.

Except he missed his mother.
He lay completely still
and tried to remember her planting
the garden below the hill.

Somewhere men were sawing wood.
Somewhere his brothers played.
Davey lay on the unmowed grass
and listened to the wind.

The cedars made a flying sound
and robins swam through the air.
How would it be to fly above
the world without a care?

Love, can you imagine
darting from tree to tree
and coming to rest on the tallest branch?
Wouldn't you feel free?

Davey looked up at the sky,
the long grass for his bed,

~ *Davey lay on the unmowed grass* ~

the white clouds sailing high above,
but still he was sad.

His eyes were growing lazy
till all of him felt light
as if he were floating above the hill,
alone and remote.

And then the strangest feeling
came over our boy on the grass
as if it grew out of the hillside
and came to pass.

A Fence Almost as Tall as the Sky

He saw men building a fence
almost as tall as the sky.
They nailed the upright lumber in place
and Davey knew he could fly.

He heard the hammers tapping,
saw crossbeams nailed to the posts
and rows of two-by-fours rose up
like a thousand sailing masts.

His father and Mr. Larsen
mumbled together like bees.
The smell of wood and tobacco
crossed on a tossing breeze.

And the fence rose over the garden
and over the rolling hill.
Almost as high as the cedars
lay its highest rail.

Davey took hold of a vertical plank
and began to shinny up.
He wedged his feet between the boards
and aimed toward the top

till the hill lay far below him,
the garden and the grass.
Davey sat on top of the fence,
his beating heart at peace.

He could see the house by the lake,
more houses toward the town,
and birds flew by to look at him
on the fence's crown.

Slowly our Davey stood up.
He was happy through and through
because his heart felt light as a bird
and he knew what he had to do.

First Flight

He spread his arms and jumped!
Just when he thought he would fall,
the wind rushed up to hold him
and he could sail.

What joy!
The wind blew warm on his face
and whooshed in his ears
and held him in place

till he learned to steer himself forward
with a simple nod of his head,

and bank his body to make a turn.
He learned he could read the wind

by watching the waving trees
and the darker waves on the lake
and the happy, paddling ducks.
What incredible luck!

He had never known he could fly,
and all by using his brain.
Whenever he thought he might fall
he just thought his way up again.

At first he stayed close to home,
circling the house.
His father and Mr. Larsen waved
so he sailed down close.

"I'm flying!" he shouted.
"Well done!" they said.
And neither man looked worried at all
so Davey nodded his head

and soared up over the cedars
and banked down over the shore.
He flew over trout in the water
and back to the garden once more,

and over the woods to the waterfall
with its bed of mossy stone.
He dove close to look for the peacock,
but it was gone.

So he sailed toward town
over the houses of neighbors.
He saw Mrs. Larsen look up at him
from her garden labors.

~ *he sailed toward town* ~

"It's good to see you, Davey.
I see you can fly—what fun!
Don't wear yourself out and please don't fly
too close to the sun!"

"I promise I'll be careful."
But Davey liked to try
experimenting with his mind
to see what he could be.

He could think himself into falling
and think himself back to the air
and tumble around like a wind-blown cloud
without a single care.

And then he smelled the dew
warm on the sunlit grass
and knew what he had to do.
He had to wake up at last.

The Earth Felt Heavy

Love, have you ever had a dream
that seemed more real than your life?
Davey lay on the grassy hill
and tried to lift himself off,

but his body felt so heavy,
his arms and legs too hard,
as if he were not a little boy
but a puppet made of lead.

His father and Mr. Larsen
were digging the fencepost holes,
leaving little mounds of dirt
like burrowing moles.

"Davey McGravy," his father said.
"Taking a nap, I see.
No harm in that, I guess.
Especially on Saturday.

"Why don't you tell your brothers
to come outside and play?
Or help me carry those boards up here?
What do you say?"

Davey walked on the grass,
now dry where the sun had shone.
He felt so strange and heavy
and utterly alone.

It's hard on a boy who has flown
to feel the weight of things
when all around him the robins
keep on singing

and the clouds go flying freely
and the trees rise up as before.
Davey walked down to the house by the lake
and opened the screen door.

"Don't Say That"

Big Brother sat by his model,
a battleship painted gray.
Little Brother sat nearby on the floor,
muttering at play.

"I think I can fly," our Davey said,
but now he wasn't so sure.
His brothers turned to look at him
and the room began to blur.

"Don't say that," Big Brother said.
Little Brother sucked his thumb.
"You can't say crazy things like that,"
both brothers said. "It's dumb."

So Davey kept it to himself,
the way he climbed the fence and flew,
the way the wind rushed up to catch him.
He knew what he knew.

The things that happened in his mind
and things that happened in the day
happened together like a rhyme.
And he could fly!

Supper!

That night they had meatloaf,
potatoes and green beans,
and sat around the table,
a motherless family.

"With Larsen's help," their father said,
"we'll finish the fence tomorrow.
I was glad to have you carry those boards."
He tried to hide his sorrow—

their mother had planted the beans
and everything else in the garden.
Big Brother looked at Davey
and his eyes began to harden.

"Dumbbell says he can fly," Big Brother said.
Little Brother said, "So dumb."

Davey ate his dinner
but felt his heart go numb.

"He flew down the rolling hill,"
their father said. "I saw him."
And that was when the sky outside
broke open in a storm.

Thunder rattled the windows
and raindrops hammered the roof.
Davey was quiet. He knew he could fly
though he had no proof.

Night Flight

The storm crashed on for hours
while Davey lay in bed
and felt the whole house tossing
but he didn't feel dread.

Instead he thought himself free,
and flew into the night
and banked above the darkened forest
lightninged with delight.

The rain blew into his face.
He skimmed the tallest trees
so their needles scratched his belly.
He flew with the greatest of ease,

and when the storm abated
the bats came out to greet him
using their radar, flying blind,
and squeaking and bleating,

~ *"Welcome to our night, little boy!"* ~

"Welcome to our night, little boy!
Watch us eat our supper,
clearing the air of mosquitoes!
We're super-duper!"

Davey closed his eyes
and flew blind like the bats,
and the wind grew still and stars came out
and he opened his eyes and that's

when he saw the path of moonlight
leading over the lake,
and he shouted "Mother, I can fly!
I'm flying for your sake.

Just tell me where you've gone,
whether you're near or far.
I'll fly until I find you
no matter where you are."

"We'll help," said the bats.
"You're blind," said Davey.
"But blindness doesn't matter," they squeaked,
"when you're Davey McGravy.

"You can dream yourself over the water,
and over the lights of the town
and out to the distant islands
or anywhere you've flown.

"You can fly by your nose or radar.
You can steer by your mind and the stars.
And when the sun comes back through the clouds
you'll be past the farthest farms."

And Davey sailed on through the night.
His heart was lighter than air.

And Love, that's where we'll leave him—
soaring without a care.

And if you dream tonight
don't let it end too soon.
Let the blind bats keep you company
by the light of the moon.

The Music in the Mall

Time Flies

Love, can you think of what else flies?
Time does. Doesn't it?
Time goes by so fast, and blind
as a bat—wasn't it?

Time on the lake went waving by
the green house and the trees,
time like a high cloud in the sky
pushed by a speedy breeze.

Suddenly it was Saturday
all over again. The fence
was finished at the garden patch,
but where the whole week went

Davey couldn't say. "Time to get up,"
his father said. "It's a shopping day."
But Davey had flown all night in his dreams
and wanted to stay asleep
and wanted to keep the bats as friends
and the voice of his mother that never ends
and the rain on the moon
and the grass of the sun
though it grew too soon.
It was all such fun.

"Davey McGravy," his father said,
and reached to touch his hair.
"Time to get up, you sleepyhead.
Pancakes are waiting downstairs."

Pancakes! Davey flew to his clothes,
pulled on his jeans, his socks and his shoes

and ran downstairs
and leapt on his chair.

The smell of bacon filled the air
and even Big Brother smiled.
Little Brother came to the table too,
his hair all sleepy-wild.

And the family ate and was happy to eat
with maple syrup, warm and sweet,
and their father rubbed his whiskers and said
he knew what would get them out of bed.

Going to Town

They crammed into the pick-up cab
and drove the road to town.
Suddenly cars were everywhere
and buildings all around.

They passed the library—quiet now.
They passed the harbor boats.
They passed the churches and the place
their father went to vote.

They passed the courthouse and museum,
a playground and a school.
They passed the skateboard park, and next
a kid-filled swimming pool.

And then—

The Mall!

—then they were at the mall!
The parking lot was like a field
growing a crop of cars.
It was too big to be real.

"Now stick together," their father said.
"I don't want you getting lost.
We'll get you shoes and clothes for school,
before you see Jack Frost."

Little Brother rode on father's back.
Big Brother ran ahead.
Davey McGravy looked about him,
and thoughts flew through his head.

Inside the mall was like a forest
of stores and moving stairs,
with waterfalls and plastic palms
and a ceiling of glittering stars.

There were shops for shoes and shops for jeans,
shops for guitars and tambourines,
shops for balls and skis and dresses,
a man showing how to clean up messes
with a magic mop. An ice cream shop,
a pizza bar, a strolling cop,
a raffle car, shops for cooking . . .
Davey stood there, looking and looking.

"Keep up with us," Big Brother said.
"First we're getting shoes.
If you don't keep up with the rest of us,
you lose!"

"Okay, partner," their father said,
and let Little Brother down.
But Davey was looking across the mall
at a performing clown.

"Come on, McG," his father said.
"Let's try the shoes in here."
They stepped into a bright orange store
with shoes arranged in tiers.

Davey's mind was far away
where a high call came to his ears,
a distant call, a familiar call:
"Here. I'm here. I'm here."

The Call in the Mall

There were so many sounds to hear:
music from all the stores,
crowds of people walking by,
the waterfall as high as the sky
with its glittering plastic stars.

Father had three boys to watch,
and it was hard to see
with so many sights to focus on,
and Davey just drifted away.

He didn't think of getting lost,
like losing a trail in the woods.
He just started walking past the stores,
looking at all the goods,

the forest of girls and boys with bags
of all the stuff they'd bought,

old folks in wheelchairs or with canes—
it was a lot
for a boy with brains to see.

And the popcorn-burger-hotdog smell,
the perfume smell as well,
and all the names of stores to spell,
and then there came that call:

"Here. I'm here. I'm here," it said
from somewhere far away.
Is it a peacock in my head
calling me out to play?

Mother!

And then he saw her in the crowd—
Mother!—walking ahead.
Love, do you know what it's like to see
someone you feared was dead?

It had to be her. The hair was her,
the dress, the way she walked
like a woman drifting in a fog.
If only she'd turn and talk!

Davey ran as fast as he could
but the mall was packed with people.
All he could see was the crazy clown
juggling with four apples,

and then that hair again, that walk
to the escalator going up—
past the waterfall, toward the stars—
up, up, up, up—

"Mommy!" he shouted. People stopped
to stare at our boy Davey.
An old man touched his arm and asked,
"Son, are you okay?"

But Davey ran as he had never run,
not in the rain and not in the sun.
He ran past all the arms and knees
of all the people, the plastic trees,

and took the escalator up—
up, up, up, up—
the moving staircase to the stars
to another floor of glittering stores.

"Mommy!" he shouted. People stared.
Where was the hair and where the walk?
Where was the one he wanted to talk to,
to hold him in her arms?

And was that her? He looked ahead,
saw someone enter a store,
and that was when he heard again:
"Here. I'm here! I'm here!"

The Bird of a Word

It had to be her! He ran to the store
and stood at the door and looked—
the smell of animals everywhere.
He saw cages that were locked,

aquariums of clownfish,
coral castles, octopi,

a hutch of rabbits on the floor,
a cat with multi-colored eyes.

He saw a litter of tiny pups
still suckling their mother.
He saw some gerbils, Guinea pigs
that nuzzled with each other.

It was a universe of pets,
animals from everywhere,
of stinks and squeals and flutters and fins—
he stared and stared and stared.

He saw three different kinds of snake,
some lizards, a horny toad,
and from the cages hung above
came birdsong like the sound of love,

tweets and twitters, coos and calls,
piccolo trills that filled the walls.
A white bird with a yellow crown
looked down on him—and he

looked up and met the white bird's eyes.
The bird seemed totally unsurprised.
Davey was getting used to this
when he met the world with openness.

"I told you I was here," said the bird.
"Did you see her?" Davey said.
The bird said, "You're the boy who flies
whenever he dreams in bed."

"I saw my mother. I think I did."
Davey looked all through the store
but the only woman he could see
showed pups to a customer.

~ *"I'm free," said the hopping cockatoo* ~

He felt his heart fall to the floor.
He looked at the bird and the bird looked back,
blurred by tears,
and made a squawk.

"I'm here," said the bird. "I'm always here,
though I came from far away.
It's tough on an Australian cockatoo
in the good old U. S. A.

"But enough about me. I see you're sad,
and if you watch me dance
it'll teach you a thing or two about life
you can learn at a glance."

Dance in a Cage

With that the cockatoo raised up
one foot from her perching bar
and hopped onto the other foot
and back and forth some more.

She shook her yellow crown and whistled
a song from far away,
and Davey watched with tears in his eyes
the dance inside a cage.

"I'm free," said the hopping cockatoo,
"as long as I can dance.
Like you I fly all night in my dreams.
I whistle and shriek and laugh and scream
like a girl with ants in her pants!
These other birds think I'm absurd.
It doesn't matter what they say.

I'm like a kid with a rhyming name,
lost in the woods but all the same
I still know how to play!"

And Davey began to bend his knees
and lift his feet from the floor,
and his heart rose up as he moved in a dance
so he danced and danced some more.

The people in the store turned to see
the boy and the dancing bird,
and it didn't matter a bit to Davey
whether they thought him absurd.

They danced to the yapping puppy dogs.
They danced to the finning fish.
They danced to the pink-eyed rabbits and
they danced all they could wish.

They danced to the lizards, danced to the snakes,
danced to the parrots, danced to the dove,
hopped and wiggled and
squawked for love

till Davey fell on the floor with a laugh
and the cockatoo bowed down,
and Davey was glad he had come that day
with his family into town.

"You're a plucky boy," the white bird said.
"Come see me again, my friend,
and we'll dance some more, and maybe you'll see
your mother again.

"That's all I can say about life, my boy.
I live in a cage, as you see,

and dance when I think of my own broken heart
and my far country."

Davey stood and thanked the bird
and bowed to the people who thought him absurd
and turned to the door in time to see
his father and brothers—one, two, three!

The Hug

"Davey McG," his father said.
"You gave me quite a scare.
I should have guessed you'd find this store.
We've looked for you everywhere."

Big Brother shook his head. "You see?
I told you he'd get lost."
Little Brother sucked his thumb and said,
"How much does a puppy cost?"

Davey turned to look once more
at the nodding cockatoo,
and nodding back, our Davey McGravy
knew what he had to do.

He hugged his father by the legs.
His father knelt and hugged him back.
"You're quite the explorer. I always find you
off the beaten track."

And then his father stood and saw
the white bird with her crown.
He touched the whiskers of his face
and he didn't frown.

"Beautiful bird," his father said.
"Is that a cockatoo?
I never saw one of those before
except in a zoo."

"She can dance and sing," our Davey said.
His father touched the bars
of the cage, and the bird bowed down
and nipped at his fingers

but still he didn't frown.
"Well, we can't linger
here all day. Come on, you clowns,
let's get the shopping done."

Supper and Bed

That night they had pizza
and got to watch TV.
Davey didn't tell anyone
who he thought he'd seen.

He didn't say what the bird had said
or sung from far away,
and when he climbed upstairs for bed
the whole day swimming in his head
was like a kind of play.

He saw the woman in the crowd,
then saw her disappear.
He saw the dancing cockatoo
and his vision blurred.

He saw the stars and waterfall.
He rode the flowing stairs.

He bowed to the bird and she bowed back
and danced away her cares.

On his bed were the jeans he got for school,
and on the floor were his shoes,
and in the closet hung new shirts
of forest hues.

But his mind was dancing in a cage
to a song from far far off:
Davey McGravy, Davey McGravy,
a name to conjure with.

It sounds like rain on a window.
It sounds like wind in the trees.
It sounds like a fern in the forest
dancing in the breeze.

The Rule in School

A Cold Touch

Love, have you ever seen Jack Frost?
No? I haven't either.
But some days you wake up and find
a change in the weather.

Davey woke up one day and heard
a whisper in the air,
as if a colder daylight came
quietly up the stairs.

Something about the sound of waves
beyond the house on the lake.
Something about the giants' boots,
something about the ducks,

something about the squeaky geese
in an arrow flying south.
He stepped outside and tasted change,
a chill in his mouth.

That day when he walked to the waterfall
he saw the spawning fish
struggling to swim upstream.
"This is hard work," their faces said.
"Sometimes we wish
we could stay on the bed
of the lake and dream."

He saw the mist rise out of the trees
like smoke from an ancient fire.
He followed the mossy waterfall
higher and higher,

wanting to say goodbye
to any peacock he might meet,
or huckleberry shrub or spider.
Something was incomplete.

But nobody called his name that day.
Nobody said, "I'm here."
All the voices had gone away
as if they never were.

Davey went home and sat inside,
and played with his brothers
but wanted to hide
and never come out of his hiding place.
Whatever bird or word he wanted
seemed to have been erased.

The Yellow Bus

Love, in the land of rain
and the tallest of tall trees
children waiting for a bus
wear raincoats to their knees.

Their father waited with them,
out on the edge of the road.
"Nice weather," he liked to joke,
"that is, if you're a toad!"

But Davey loved the rain
pattering on his hat.
He loved to splash in the puddles,
a regular water-rat.

Big Brother checked his lunchbox
to make sure it stayed dry.
Little Brother thought of preschool
and started to cry.

He couldn't ride the bus that day
but had to go with their father
and had to play with other kids
who would tease him
for sucking his thumb,
tease him without a reason,
and tell him he was dumb.

"It's okay, partner," their father said.
He held Little Brother's hand.
"Bout time that school bus came along.
It's raining to beat the band."

And at his words the school bus rose
as if by a magic spell,
lumbering around the corner
and up the gentle hill.

Davey looked at his father,
who touched his rain-wet hat.
He looked at the open door of the bus
and the driver inside, and that

was when he felt like crying,
but he kept his tears inside.
He knew he was a plucky boy
and had no need to hide.

The bus was full of kids
who lived along the shore,

and as it moved along the road
it picked up more and more.

Big Brother sat with a boy his age
and Davey sat alone
till a girl named Alice sat with him
and showed him her cell phone.

With twenty squirming kids on board,
shouting and laughing together,
the driver hunched at the wheel and peered
out at the weather,

the wipers beating time in the rain,
children bobbing on seats and again
Davey thought of the mall,
he thought of the waterfall
and everything so loud,
the woman in the crowd,
the dancing cockatoo
in its cage like a bird in a zoo,
and leaned his head on the window glass
and let the time go past.

Mean Boys

"I heard you think you can fly," said a voice.
Davey looked up and saw
a boy named Jasper on the seat in front
who had a jutting jaw.

He looked at Alice who looked at her phone.
He felt so clumsy and all alone.
"Your brother says you think you can fly.
You're crazy. Bet I can make you cry."

Jasper reached from the seat in front
to slap at Davey's face,
but Davey dodged the slap
and stayed there in his place,

so Jasper made a fist and punched
and Davey stood to punch him back,
but Alice pulled him to the seat
before he could attack.

"Don't listen to him," Alice said.
"And you, leave him alone."
Davey looked at her in wonder.
She looked at her phone.

"Davey thinks he can fly," said Jasper.
"Davey thinks he can fly.
Dumbbell thinks he can jump off a roof.
Bet I can make him cry!"

Another boy in the back of the bus
called, "Davey thinks he can fly.
Dumbbell thinks he can jump off a roof.
Bet we can make him cry."

"Now that's enough," the driver said.
"You boys simmer down.
I'll stop the bus if I have to
before we get to town."

"Davey thinks he can fly," sang the boys.
"Davey thinks he can fly.
Davey thinks he can jump off a roof.
Bet we can make him cry!"

"Stop," said Alice. "Stop it now!"
The two boys quit their song.
"Don't listen to those jerks," she said,
and sighed. "It won't be long."

The town rose up around them now,
the park with the drained swimming pool,
the buildings and the harbor boats.
Then they were at school.

Mrs. Pickle and the Words That Rhyme

Love, that was a hard way to start
the first day of school.
Davey sat close to Alice in class
but felt like a little fool.

Their teacher was Mrs. Pickle.
Of course they laughed at her name
but quietly, and they listened
as she played a spelling game.

And then she taught the subject
that made our Davey feel sick
because it was so hard for him:
arithmetic.

But Alice loved all numbers
the way she loved her phone,
and showed how numbers were a group
yet single and alone.

The best part of the morning
was story-time, of course.
They sat on the floor and Mrs. Pickle
told of the flying horse

called Pegasus, and how the Greeks
thought poetry could fly like that.
Some poems had words that rhymed.
Davey was rapt.

Mrs. Pickle read a poem
by Robert Louis Stevenson,
and Davey McGravy felt the day
was finally going to be okay:

"All by myself I have to go,
With none to tell me what to do—
All alone beside the streams
And up the mountain-sides of dreams.

"The strangest things are there for me,
Both things to eat and things to see,
And many frightening sights abroad,
Till morning in the Land of Nod."

He could feel the touch of words, the breath,
light as a dewy spider web
or voices heard on a forest trail.
Outside the room it began to hail

and he watched the schoolyard grass go white
and felt his heart at last as light
as words that tumbled out of air.
Davey McGravy. Davey McGravy.
He rhymed himself, our wavy Davey,
and even if he had to fight
the bullies again, he didn't care.

Recess!

By the time they went outside to play
the hail had melted, the sky was clear.
Davey climbed the monkey bars
and hung without a trace of fear

and shouted to Alice, "You're upside down!"
and dropped to the gravel on the ground.

But there a pair of boots he knew
were waiting for him.
It was Jasper and his crew
in a mood for warring.

Davey stood up, ready to fight
"Here's the boy who thinks he can fly,"
said Jasper, jeering.
"Let's see if we can make him cry."

A boy kicked Davey in the knee.
Jasper stamped on his toes
and socked him in the arm
to make him come to blows.

"Davey thinks he can fly," sang the boys
"Davey thinks he can fly.
Davey thinks he can jump off a roof.
Bet we can make him cry!"

"Stop," Alice screamed. "Please stop!"
But the boys were gleeful now.
Their eyes were burning and their fists
were ready to come to blows.

Davey felt his face go red.
He held up his hands to fight,
but someone else was shouting, "Enough!
It isn't right!"

And: "Leave my little brother alone.
Leave him alone, I said."
Big Brother stepped into their midst,
swinging his arms as he went.

~ *He held up his hands to fight* ~

"Whoa," said Jasper. "Jeeze," said the boys.
"We were just having fun."
"Enough of your fun," Big Brother said.
"You're done."

The mean boys backed away
behind the monkey bars.
Big Brother stood there panting.
His face was hard.

He looked at Davey and seemed to see
something he'd never seen before.
"They give you trouble, come to me."
And he walked to the school door.

Davey stood in the schoolyard,
watching his brother go.
Alice was almost crying,
but why, he didn't know.

The mean boys circled the gravel,
blocking his way to the door.
Davey decided he'd better leave
and be alone once more.

The Harbor Gulls

He ran from the school as fast as he could,
past the fence and across the road,
ran on the sidewalk, wind in his ears.
Davey knew he was odd.

He knew that school didn't fit him,
or he didn't fit in school.

He felt like a boy who'd broken
some unspoken rule.

Did Alice call out his name?
He thought he heard her voice
behind him in the schoolyard,
but he had made his choice.

He'd run away for good.
He'd run away to the sea.
He'd climb aboard a fishing boat
and flee and flee and flee.

He'd sail out to the islands.
He'd live alone in a tent.
He'd talk to fish and killer whales
and gulls and cormorants.

And now he was at the harbor,
smelling of fish and kelp,
and knew no one would find him
or offer any help.

Davey was alone again,
alone as he could be.
He walked by the docks and fishing boats,
looking out to sea.

"Ow," said a voice above him.
"Ow," another cried.
"You sure don't look like the little boy
who thinks he can fly."

Two seagulls sailed above his head.
They floated there in place,
enjoying an updraft from the bay.
"My, what a sad face."

"Are you the boy with the rhyming name?"
said a gull with gray on its wing.
"Word travels far among the birds,
especially those who sing."

"You're not alone," said the second gull.
"We're always here," said the first.
"We know all about hunger.
We know all about thirst.

"We know all about pain,
crying 'Ow!' all day
at the garbage scow and the fishing boats.
'Ow' is the word we say."

"It's in our natures," the second said.
"It's our favorite word," said the first.
"It's a pretty mournful comedy,
but it could be worse!"

"Ow!" said Davey.
"Ow!" said the gulls.
"He looks like a boy
who's broken the rules."

"Can you fly?" said the first. "It helps
to fly when you're sad."
"That's why people laugh at me,"
said Davey. "They think I'm mad,

"but I only fly when I'm asleep
and dreaming.
It's just a way I let the world
go on seeming."

"Ow!" said the gulls. "If you fall asleep
you can fly with us all day.

We know a really good garbage heap
where we can play."

Davey sat on a dock and leaned
on a coil of weathered rope,
and felt his eyes go heavy,
ready for a nap.

And that was when—

Into the Air

You guessed it, Love—he flew!
He thought himself into the air
among the gulls, and knew
he could fly without a care.

"Let's go to the school," he said.
"Let's show them I can fly."
"No," said the gulls, "don't let them see.
Be secret in the sky."

The first gull said, "Now tip your arms
and bank low over the waves."
The second gull said, "Now follow us
and watch how seagulls play."

They flew together over the docks,
over the fishing boats,
over the waves, over the rocks,
over the yachts and floats.

They flew to a garbage mound
where dozens of gulls were flying around
enjoying the garbage smell.
They flew in a whirling whirl.

~ They flew to a garbage mound ~

Davey could see the objects below,
things he had seen in the mall—
shoes and clothes and furniture
in a heap that was so tall

it would take him a day to climb it.
All the thrown-out things:
food, deflated balls and toys
and even kitchen sinks.

"We're rich," said the gulls. "Just look at this stuff!
And people throw it away!
We fly out here to meet our friends
and eat and play all day."

"I'd rather eat trout," our Davey said,
"even when they look sad."
"We're omnivorous," said the gulls.
"There's nothing that tastes bad!"

"Davey," a voice said in his ear.
"Davey," it said again.
"Davey McGravy," said a deep voice.
"Come on, old friend."

A hand lay on his shoulder.
He woke up on the dock,
blinking eyes at his father.
It was quite a shock!

Found

"I'm glad I found you, Davey,"
his father knelt and said.
"I'd be mighty sad if you hurt yourself
or ended up dead."

"How?" said Davey, rubbing his eyes.
"I got a call," said his father.
"Alice's mother said she'd had
a phone call from her daughter.

"Told me about some trouble at school.
Told me you'd run away.
I drove here lickety-split, old chum.
We've both had quite a day.

"And it looks like you've had quite a sleep.
I drove around for hours.
Should have known you'd take a nap
somewhere near the water.

"Come on, son," his father said.
"I'll take you back to school.
They don't like boys who run away—
against the rules."

"They hate me there," our Davey said.
"Not everyone," said his father.
Davey held his father's leg
and felt much calmer.

"Davey McGravy, Davey McGravy.
No one's got a name like you.
It won't be easy, going back.
We'll see what we can do."

That Night

Love, it was not the end of tears,
or even the end of fighting.
But Davey knew he was not alone.
He had a friend with a telephone
and a brother who was trying.

That night he flew into the rain,
beyond the tears, beyond the pain,
beyond the garbage mound, the school,
beyond the park with the swimming pool,
remembering words he said for fun
from Robert Louis Stevenson:

"Try as I like to find the way,
I never can get back by day,
Nor can remember plain and clear
The curious music that I hear."

The Land of Nod, the Land of Nod—
Mother, I can fly!
I know it's a dream, but I'm flying for you,
out in the rainy sky.

And Love, if you can dream tonight,
and if you fly, don't worry.
Everything will be all right.
So take your time. Don't hurry.

Out of the Fog

Indian Summer

Love, have you ever heard the waves
lapping on the shore?
They slap and hush and suck and slap,
then lap and slap some more.

When big winds come they turn all white
and frothy-gray and rise
like mountain ranges made of water
almost to the skies.

Some days the lake was unearthly still,
quiet as the moon.
Raindrops hissed in little circles
that disappeared *so* soon.

Some days waiting for the bus
Davey watched the trees,
maples and alders letting go
of all their yellow leaves.

He watched the shaggy cedars sway
as if they were looking about,
trying to see where the giants went.
If you see them, give a shout.

Love, sometimes, going to school,
our Davey's days were hard.
The mean boys found new ways to be mean.
He wished he was a bird

and could fly at recess over the town
and find the seagulls sailing,
out to the garbage mound, the islands,
out to the fish and whales.

When the mean boys surrounded him
and said they would make him cry,
Alice showed them her cell phone,
Big Brother came to his side.

But school was a strange kind of waiting
till something clicked like a rhyme,
some story he heard, some new kind of word
that tuned him to the time.

When Mrs. Pickle, his gray-haired teacher,
could see by a change in his eyes
that Davey was happy at story-time,
she wasn't surprised.

She let him write stories as much as he wished
and said he should make a book.
He clutched his pencil and wrote his words
with a determined look.

He was glad when the Friday bus came to school
and took them back to the lake,
emptying kids at every stop
and leaving them in its wake.

On Friday night, cooking supper,
his father would ask the boys
to say what had happened at school that day
and whether it gave them joy.

One late September Friday at home
the weather was warm and muggy.
"It's Indian Summer," their father said.
"Tomorrow it might be foggy."

And Davey slept in a fog that night.
He didn't dream and he didn't fly.

He slept like a stone or a cedar tree,
slept like a shoe, like a fallen leaf,
slept like a wave that lapped the shore.
And Saturday morning he slept some more...

Thick!

The warm air met the cold air,
and fog came out of the ground,
came out of the trees, came out of the bogs
without a sound.

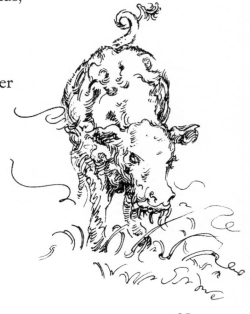

In town the streetlights' ghostly glow
was faint, and by the bay
the fog horns moaned, the ship bells rang—
you could hardly tell it was day.

Fog settled over valley roads.
It drifted, slowly looped
around barns and cows in the fields,
thicker than pea soup.

Even dogs got lost in the fog.
Fishermen had another grog,
sat waiting for a change of weather
on a silver driftwood log.

Was it day or was it night?
Was it wrong or was it right?
Was it summer, was it fall?
Fog had settled over all,

fog that smelled of cedar woods,
fog that smelled of salty air,

fog that smelled of hay and rain,
fog that smelled of tar.

Roads were empty, no one moved
in the land of rain and trees.
No engines started. No one coughed.
There wasn't the slightest breeze.

Davey woke to a smell in his room,
a fog of bacon from downstairs.
Groggy with sleep, he rose and dressed
and joined his brothers for breakfast.

Their father looked at his boys and laughed.
Their hair stood up, their eyes were shut.
They chewed their food and swallowed it down,
but none of them could wake up.

"What do you do," their father said,
"on a foggy day like this?
Play in the yard, stay close to the house,
or sit inside, I guess."

But Davey's ears had opened now.
He could hear the fog on the roof,
the fog at the windows, out on the lawn . . .
His brothers were still deaf

and blind from a night of foggy sleep.
Davey was waking now.
He washed his plate at the kitchen sink
and asked if he could go out.

"Put a jacket on," his father said,
"and don't go far away."
So Davey pulled on his coat and boots,
and stepped into the day.

The Voices

The day was white as an empty page,
then out came a cedar limb,
and a massive tree rose up in the mist
and Davey began to climb.

The bark was rough, but the limbs came down
and helped him into the air.
He climbed into the cloudy green,
but couldn't see anywhere,

so he sat on a branch and felt it sway
and thought he could stay up here all day
till he heard a flutter of wings.

A crow had settled just above,
watching him with the darkest love.
"Come along," it said. "Come along."

"I'm not supposed to leave the yard,"
said Davey. Clearing its throat,
the crow said, "Come. Come along.
It isn't at all remote."

"What isn't remote? Where will we go?"
But the crow said, "Come.
And the fog said, "Come."
And the dewy grass and the day said, "Come."

"Into the fog," the voices said.
"Don't be afraid. You're not alone.
Remember your friend with the telephone.
Remember your brother is not so mean.
Remember everywhere you've been.
Remember who you are
and come with us. It isn't far."

And Davey climbed down from the tree
and stood on the earth, mist all around,
and followed the crow without a sound
as it flew ahead and waited.
"Come along," it said. "Come along with me."

The day felt dark and haunted,
but Davey walked and followed the crow
as it moved from limb to limb.
They were headed for the waterfall
in the woods that whispered, "Come."

~ A crow had settled just above ~

Watched

I won't get lost. I know the way,
thought Davey. *I'll get home*
in time for supper and for bed.
I know I'm not alone.

But Love, there was a ghost of fear
in his bones as he walked the trail,
keeping his eyes on the darting crow
as it fanned its blue-black tail.

The ferns and nettles dripped with dew.
His jeans were wet now, through and through,
and the air was like a foggy stew,
but Davey knew what he had to do.

Just a little bit further and I'll see
what's around the bend, he thought.
Just one more tree beyond the next tree.
The crow gave a hawking cough

to clear its throat. "Ahem," it said,
"keep coming along.
You know the place we're going to.
You know it won't be long."

Out of the fog the gashing thorns
of blackberries rose in tangles.
Old rotting trunks lay across the trail
at crazy angles.

But Davey followed the darting crow
around the bends and up the trail.
Over the stumps, across the rocks
he followed the fanning tail.

And suddenly he had a thought
clear at the back of his mind—
he wasn't alone as he followed the crow.
There was someone else behind.

He stood on the trail and listened a while,
but no sound came to meet him.
So he walked until he found the crow
that cleared its throat in greeting.

The thought came back. This time it came
to the front of his mind like lightning.
He wasn't alone. His hair stood up.
Davey was frightened.

He stopped again. He listened hard.
Nothing. Again there was nothing.
He looked at the impatient crow.
Nothing, nothing, nothing.

No twig snapped, no creature breathed,
or moved on the trail behind.
Nothing moved above or ahead.
He stood as if deaf and blind,

and the hair stood out on his neck and arms
and he felt his skin go cold.
Someone is watching, Davey thought.
Let's get to the waterfall.

The Meeting

He could hear the falling stream ahead,
muffled by fog and moss.
At the waterfall he found the big log
and started across,

but saw no peacock in the trees
and no fish in the stream.
The foggy clearing in the woods
was silent as a dream.

The crow stood by the waterfall.
"Why have we come?" asked Davey.
"We came because you are the boy
named Davey McGravy.

"Remember who you are," said the crow.
"Remember the things that rhyme,
like two sides of a leaf, like rain.
Remember the time."

"We're not alone," our Davey said,
"so why am I afraid?"
And then the fog began to lift
from the waterfall in the glade,

and Davey felt his prickling skin,
the hair on the back of his neck.
He tried to balance on the log
as he looked from rock to rock—

and there she was, above him,
not thirty feet away,
a crouching mountain lioness.
Davey began to sway

but caught himself before he fell
and clung to the mossy trunk.
He looked again. She was still there,
above him on a rock.

The crow said not a word, but watched
as boy and lion met.
Davey was shaking and holding on,
so cold and wet.

I'm going to die, he thought. *I know
I'm going to die.*
"You'll see," said the mind-reading crow.
"I brought you here to see."

Davey knew he could perish then,
knew he could disappear,
knew they would say he was lost in a fog
for ever and ever.

He thought of his father looking for him,
Big Brother at his side,
of Little Brother sucking his thumb
who might even cry.

This is the way you die, he thought.
All alone in the woods.
He thought of the rotten trees on the trail.
He thought of the tangled roots.

And the lioness crouched above him
watching him silently.
And when she stood and made a move,
Davey knew he would die.

The Lioness

Her paws were bigger than cooking pots,
her head was huge and tawny.
Her eyes were darker than the fog
as she moved on her slow haunches.

Behind her a tail rose like a rope,
swishing in the air.
Her huge form waded into the stream.
Davey trembled and stared.

He knew she would pounce. He knew her jaws
could break him in two if she wished.
She waded slowly toward him,
and her tail went *swish*.

Soon she was nearly beside him,
in water, under the log.
Davey clung to the mossy bark
and saw her breath like a fog.

"Come along," said the crow. "Come along."
Alighting on her head,
it gazed at Davey as if to say,
"Nobody's dead."

The lioness looked up at him
and what shone in her eyes
was not a murderous hunger or hate.
Davey was surprised.

He saw she meant for him to climb
onto her tawny back.
She seemed to have sought him in the woods
only for his sake.

"Come," said the crow. "Come," said the air.
"Come," said the forest everywhere.
"There's nothing to fear, nothing to fear.
The fog is lifting, the day is clear."

Davey felt his hair lie down.
He nodded at the crow,
let go and slid from the tree trunk
to the lioness below.

He felt the muscles of her back,
smelled forest fog from her fur.
And when she moved her great slow limbs
the crow said, "It isn't far."

~ *The boy, the crow and the lioness* ~

The House by the Lake

The fog rose out of the woods
like smoke from an ancient fire.
Blackberries thorned in the sunlight.
Hills rose higher and higher.

The boy, the crow and the lioness
moved through woods still dripping,
ferns and nettles and bright salal,
the long tail swishing.

Davey held the scruff of her neck
and she made a purring growl.
But no word came from the lioness.
She didn't smile or snarl.

Instead she moved as if asleep,
a creature in a dream.
Davey heard the distant sound
of waterfall and stream,

and then he heard the lapping waves,
the sigh of time on the lake,
and smelled the smoke from his father's stove,
and knew he was in luck.

At the road the lioness set him down,
nuzzled him gently, pushed him away.
She turned to the woods from which she'd come.
There was nothing more to say.

"I'm done," said the crow, who leapt in the air
and flew to a distant bough.
And Davey McGravy crossed the road
and entered his father's house.

The End of Day

Big Brother sat on the living room floor,
staring at TV.
Little Brother sucked his thumb and made
a noise like a drowsy bee.

Their father was reading the paper
when Davey came inside.
"Hey, McGravy, how 'bout a hug?"
And Davey clung to his thigh.

The rest of that day was quiet.
Nobody said a word
till nearly bedtime when Davey said
to his father, "I saw her."

They were alone in the kitchen.
His father was making tea,
and paused to look at his son and ask,
"Just who did you see?"

"In the mall," said Davey. "I think I did.
In the crowd, just walking there."
His father nodded. "I know what you mean.
I see her everywhere."

He knelt down in the kitchen,
held Davey in his arms.
Davey could feel his whiskers,
his father's shirt so warm.

"Davey McGravy. Time for bed.
I'll tuck you in tonight.
Now brush your teeth and wash your face.
You look a sight."

And Love, that's where we'll leave them,
in the green house by the lake,
in the land of rain and tall, tall trees
where birds go swimming in the breeze
and fish fly in the waves,

where seagulls ply the garbage mound,
where little boys are lost and found,
and even in a cage can dance
with cockatoos who take a chance,
and learn at last how they can bless
the peacock, crow and lioness.

Some days happy, some days sad,
Davey McGravy's not alone.
Just think of all the friends he's had—
like Alice with her telephone.